A Quest in
Time

Frieda Wishinsky
Illustrated by **Bill Slavin**

Owl

Owl Books are published by Greey de Pencier Books Inc.
70 The Esplanade, Suite 400, Toronto, Ontario M5E 1R2

The Owl colophon is a trademark of Owl Children's Trust Inc.
Greey de Pencier Books Inc. is a licensed user of trademarks of Owl Children's
Trust Inc.

Distributed in the United States by Firefly Books (U.S.) Inc.
230 Fifth Avenue, Suite 1607, New York, NY 10001

We acknowledge the financial support of the Canada Council for the Arts, the
Ontario Arts Council, and the Government of Canada through the Book
Publishing Industry Development Program (BPIDP) for our publishing activities.

Dedication
For my friend Shari Siamon
– F. W.

For Charolotte
– B. S.

Cataloguing in Publication Data

Wishinsky, Frieda
      A quest in time

ISBN 1-894379-07-1 (bound)   ISBN 1-894379-08-X (pbk.)

I. Slavin, Bill   II. Title.

PS8595.I834Q47   2000   jC813'.54   C00-930720-6
PZ7.W57Qu   2000

Design & art direction: Word & Image Design Studio Inc.
Illustrations: Bill Slavin

Printed in Hong Kong

A   B   C   D   E   F

"Lisa!" called her mother from the front door. "There's a delivery for you. A big trunk. It's from. . . . Oh . . . Uncle Harold."

"Oh, Mom," said Lisa, swallowing the lump in her throat. "He must have sent it before he. . . ." She couldn't bring herself to say the word "died."

"Yes," her mother said, closing her eyes in pain. She smiled gently. "Let's put it in your room, Lisa."

They carried the heavy trunk between them down the hallway and set it on the floor by Lisa's bed.

"Why don't you take a look at it on your own," Lisa's mother said, giving her daughter a hug. "You can show me later what Uncle Harold sent you."

Lisa watched her leave, then looked down at the battered trunk. She picked up the large key that lay on top. Slowly, Lisa turned the rusty key in the lock. The trunk squeaked and groaned. Then, with a tiny click, it opened! Lisa's heart raced as she lifted the lid. The trunk was full of strange objects, and Uncle Harold's journal! On top of the journal lay a note.

My dear Lisa,

One journey ends. Another begins. Learn from what you see. Learn from what you feel.

Remember I love you.

Uncle Harold

Lisa's eyes flooded with tears. She remembered Uncle
Harold's booming voice echoing through their living room as
he told them about his archeological trips, and his green eyes
dancing as he spun a story. She remembered the strange
distant look that crossed his face, and his words the last time
she saw him.

"Lisa," he said, "we're so much alike."

Did he know it was their last time together? What did his
note mean? Why had he sent her the trunk? Lisa wiped her
eyes. Uncle Harold wouldn't want her to cry. She picked up his
journal and began to read.

May 1, 1982

Iceland

What luck! We found a wooden eye from the figurehead of a Viking
ship from around 1000 A.D. The Vikings were an amazing people. They
were fierce warriors, great sailors, and skilled navigators. Their desire for
better farmland drove them to explore new lands.

"A wooden eye?" Lisa
laughed. "What eye?"

Lisa looked in the trunk.
There it was! A strange wooden
eyeball that seemed to be staring
up at her.

Lisa picked it up. Instantly, the room began to spin.

"Stop!" she shouted. She was whirling out of control. Colors and shapes stretched and blurred. And then, as suddenly as it began, the spinning stopped.

*L*isa was not in her room. She was on a ship, a Viking ship just like the ones she'd seen in her history textbooks!

The ship was tossing and turning like a toy in a whirlpool. Lisa grabbed the wooden ship's side and clung tightly to it. Steel gray waves bashed the ship. With each wave, Lisa's stomach churned. With each wave, the dragon figurehead on the front prow plunged deep into the stormy ocean. With each wave, icy water overflowed the deck.

Up. Down. Up. Down. Lisa tried to ignore the queasy feeling rising in her throat. All around men shouted, wooden boards broke, freezing water rammed the sides of the ship.

"Help!" yelled a man, shoving Lisa aside as he ran across the deck.

"We are doomed," screamed another, his face white with terror.

And then, like the boom of a thunderclap, a tall, ruddy-faced man standing beside Lisa bellowed above the noise.

"Hold on! Do not despair! Work together. The ship will not go down."

Lisa couldn't believe it! Somehow she understood what the men were saying! But how? They must be speaking an ancient Viking language. How could she understand that?

And who was that ruddy-faced man? By the way he spoke and everyone listened, he must be the captain. But it was strange. Lisa was sure she had seen him before. But where? No! It couldn't be—or could it?

Suddenly the captain turned and stared at Lisa.

"What are you standing there for? Bail! Bail!" he commanded her.

So Lisa began to bail, but it was hard. She kept slipping and sliding as the ship tossed and turned.

And then, like a siren, a piercing scream rose above the crashing waves. Lisa spun around. The cry had come from a short man lurching unsteadily to her left. Blood was trickling down his face. He swayed and then, with a clunk, fell hard against the side of the ship.

In an instant, the captain grabbed the unconscious sailor. And not a moment too soon! A huge wave rammed the ship— a wave that surely would have catapulted the injured sailor into the angry waters. The captain lay the unconscious sailor gently on the deck and then turned to the crew.

"Bail, men! Bail, I tell you! We will not go down."

The strength and confidence in his voice injected everyone with renewed energy. Lisa and all the sailors sprung into action. The storm raged on, but the panic was gone.

And then, crack! A giant wave hit the prow like an enormous fist hitting a face. The dragon figurehead split off and smashed against the ship. Broken wooden oars flew like hail, hitting the sailors in the eyes, in the nose, in the stomach. Wails and groans filled the ship.

"Stay calm," boomed their captain. "This will pass. Soon the storm will run its course."

And, at last, it did. The waves began to calm. Blue streaks broke through the dark sky.

"We are safe!" A great cheer rose from all the sailors. "Hurrah for our captain! Hurrah for Leif Eriksson! Onward to new land!"

Leif Eriksson! That ruddy-faced captain was the famous Viking Leif Eriksson. Lisa had just learned about him in school! And here she was standing beside him on a ship in the middle of the ocean.

It was all so unbelievable! Why was she here? And where were her jeans and red T-shirt? Where did she get these itchy wool pants and this stiff tan tunic?

Not only were her clothes itchy, but cold and wet. She felt like a damp rag. But at least she was alive—not smashed to bits like that slab of wood sinking into the ocean. If it wasn't for Leif they might all have gone down.

Suddenly the ship lurched.

"Not again!" exclaimed Lisa. Luckily, this time the ship was only pummeled by a small wave. But as the wave hit, something rolled onto Lisa's foot.

Lisa picked the object up. Yikes! It was . . . a wooden eyeball! She knew that eyeball. It was the eyeball from Uncle Harold's trunk! It must have fallen off the dragon masthead.

Immediately, the ship began to spin. Colors and patterns ran into each other like spilled paint. The sounds of the ocean, the voices of Leif and the sailors' faded into an eerie quiet as Lisa spun. . . .

Lisa read on in the journal.

June 10, 1983

<u>England</u>

We've found a young English boy's cap from the mid–1100s! Life was hard in those times. After the Normans conquered England in 1066, there was unrest and fighting, until Henry II and his wife, Eleanor of Aquitaine, rose to the throne in 1154. Henry helped quell the "robber barons" who roamed England robbing, torturing, and killing. Eleanor promoted learning and the arts.

"Who wore this thing?" said Lisa aloud, looking at the brown cap.

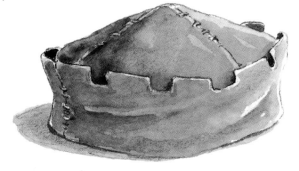

Lisa reached into the trunk and picked up the cap. Immediately, the room began to spin.

"Oh, my stomach!" said Lisa, clutching her middle. "Here we go again. . . ."

She was on a horse—a confused, agitated horse rearing in the air. Desperately, Lisa grabbed the horse's mane, but her hand slipped and she slid down and then, thump, hit the ground.

"Ow," she moaned. Luckily, she'd landed on a clump of matted leaves. But there were scratchy twigs in the clump that cut her legs right through to her leggings. Leggings! Her jeans were gone again. She was wearing a loose-fitting long skirt and rough leggings.

"Don't you know how to handle a horse?" said a boy on a gray horse staring down at Lisa.

"Not really," Lisa said. She tried to stand up but her legs hurt. "This is only the third time I've been on one."

"Well, what are you doing on a horse when you don't know how to ride?" growled the boy.

Lisa stared at the scowling boy in front of her. He was thin, about her age, wearing a long shirt, tan leggings, and a cap covering his hair.

"I'm lost," said Lisa. "Where am I?"

"You're near Salisbury," said the boy. "And you've delayed me long enough." And, with that, the boy gave his horse a kick and galloped into the forest.

"Wait! Help! Please come back," shouted Lisa. But the boy was gone. Lisa was alone in a strange forest.

"Now what do I do?" said Lisa aloud.

"Now you follow me," said the boy, laughing.

Lisa turned her head.

"You came back!" she exclaimed, relief flooding over her.

"I had to. We girls must stick together," said the other rider.

"Girls?" said Lisa. "You?"

The rider pulled off her cap and out tumbled a mass of curly brown hair.

"Yes, I'm a girl. Just like you."

"So why are you riding around looking like a boy?" asked Lisa.

"I'll tell you if you swear not to tell anyone else," said the girl.

"I swear," Lisa agreed.

"My name is Sarah," the girl began, "and I live in a village nearby. This morning, while I was waiting for my brothers' clothes to dry after I'd washed them in the river, I overheard three men planning to raid our village at dawn tomorrow. The men of our village had gone to Salisbury and there were only women and old people left. I knew we'd all be robbed and killed if someone didn't do something. There was no one else but me to get us help. I knew I had a little time. But not much."

"I still don't understand why you're wearing boy's clothes," said Lisa.

"No one pays attention to girls. As a boy I had more hope of convincing the men to help. And I was right. Ten men from a nearby village rode off immediately to help my village and should be there now, making mincemeat out of those evil marauders. And now I have to steal back, change into my real clothes, and return this horse before anyone realizes what I've done."

"Won't the people in your village be grateful you saved them?" Lisa asked.

"Ha! Grateful to a girl? I think not! Well, perhaps my mother would be, but she'd also be horrified I put my brother's clothes on and rode off like a wild boy. I pray that now that Queen Eleanor reigns with King Henry, things will be better for women. Queen Eleanor believes in learning, even for girls. She travels across the land, helping King Henry mete out justice."

Sarah looked up at the sky.

"Oh, the sun is sinking fast. I must hurry back before I am discovered and beaten for my troubles. Come." And with that, Sarah took off through a clearing in the trees.

"But. . . . But. . . ." stammered Lisa. Lisa had never galloped on a horse. But she would have to gallop to keep up with Sarah or she'd be hopelessly lost in this creepy, dark forest with night approaching.

Lisa climbed up onto the horse's back. Her heart thumped as she gave her horse a kick in the side as Sarah had done. And then, like a shot, they were off!

Lisa and her horse flew over the path through the

forest. And before she knew it, Lisa's fear vanished. She felt wonderful! She felt free! She felt fast! The sun danced through the leaves of the trees. Birds chirped a welcoming chorus. This was true magic!

Then Lisa spied Sarah in the clearing ahead, uncovering something in a pile of leaves.

"I've hidden my clothes here," said Sarah. "They're a little damp, but no worse than before. Would you hold this while I change?" And, without waiting for Lisa's reply, Sarah thrust her cap into Lisa's hands. As she did, Lisa began to spin.

"Good luck, Sarah," she managed to call, before being swept up in a twirling kaleidoscope of crazy colors and shapes.

Lisa's head was still swimming when the spinning stopped. She was back in her room, but her legs were so wobbly she could barely walk a straight line.

"I hate all this spinning. I don't even like roller coasters. I'm not touching another thing in this crazy trunk."

Lisa slammed the trunk shut and went to the kitchen to get some milk and chocolate cookies. Chocolate always made her feel better. She ate four cookies and began to calm down.

"Well, I didn't get hurt," she told herself. "And it has been amazing. Ships and storms, forests and horses! I know Uncle Harold would never send me anywhere that was dangerous. I know there's a reason for all this time travel. But what?"

Before Lisa knew it, she was racing back to her room and opening the trunk again. She picked up the journal and turned to the next page.

Life for Children in England in the mid-1100s

Life was difficult for children in the 1100s. Many families lived in small huts in one room with a fireplace in the center. Parents were strict, often beating their children if they disobeyed. Most girls lived at home, worked hard, and married young. Few girls went to school. Disease killed many people and civil disorder was rampant.

When King Henry II rose to the throne with Queen Eleanor of Aquitaine, he brought some order to England. He rid the countryside of marauders. His wife, Eleanor, was a strong-willed woman, who loved poetry and learning. But Eleanor and Henry fought bitterly, and eventually Henry kept her under arrest in a Salisbury castle for years.

"It doesn't sound as if Queen Eleanor was able to make a lot of changes," said Lisa. "Poor Sarah! Life was not much fun in those grisly days—except for riding horses. That was fun!" Lisa smiled at the memory of her exciting ride through the forest.

Then she turned to the next page in the journal. This time there was no note from Uncle Harold, just another wooden puzzle piece. It was the letter "T."

"I-T. I-T! It—what?"

Lisa read on.

July 9, 1984

<u>China</u>

What a find! A shard of a blue cup from Kublai Khan's court in China. How fine and delicate! What artistry! Marco Polo must have seen many beautiful cups like this when he lived in China in the 1270s. What marvels Marco Polo saw, such as the city of Xanadu.

Should she? Did she dare? Lisa read Uncle Harold's words again. It didn't sound as if there were any raging oceans in Xanadu. Just shining cities, beautiful palaces, and marvels. This adventure sounded fun!

Lisa picked up the shard and immediately the familiar, stomach-churning spinning began.

"Stay calm," she told herself. But, despite her attempts, the spinning still made her stomach feel queasy. Finally, it stopped.

*L*isa opened her eyes. She was wearing a richly embroidered silk robe and she was standing in a vast walled garden full of fountains and beautiful trees in bloom. Close by loomed a magnificent marble palace.

"Mmmm," she said, smelling the delicious perfume of the flowers. "This is more like it! This place is a fairyland!"

A multicolored bird strutted past Lisa.

"Hello bird! This is some place you have here," said Lisa, laughing.

"This is Shang-tu," said a man walking toward her.

"I know you," said Lisa.

"You do? I don't know you."

"You're. . . . You're. . . ."

"Marco Polo, at your service," said the man, bowing slightly.

"Wow!" said Lisa.

"How do you know my name?" Marco asked.

"I studied about you in school," Lisa blurted out.

Marco Polo stared at her as if she were crazy.

"How could you?" he said.

Lisa realized there was no way that Marco Polo would understand how she had learned about him in a twentieth-century school.

"I . . . mean . . . I heard about you from my uncle," she stammered.

"Yes, uncles love telling stories," said Marco. "If it wasn't for my uncle and my father, I wouldn't be in Cathay. Their stories made me yearn to see this wondrous place. So I joined them. We left our home in Venice and trekked through mysterious, unknown lands for three and a half years. What sights we saw! What dangers we faced! We often wondered if we'd live to see another day—let alone reach Cathay. But here we are, and here you are!"

"Cathay?" said Lisa. "Where exactly is that?"

"It's. . . . Watch out!"

Marco pushed Lisa aside. Just in time! A cabin mounted on the backs of two elephants and draped with lion skins almost knocked them both down. The cabin was followed by hundreds of men with scary looking birds perched on their

arms and other men on horseback with cheetahs mounted behind them.

"What is all this for?" Lisa asked Marco.

"The Great Kublai Khan, Emperor of Cathay, and his men," said Marco.

"Where is he going?"

"On a hunting expedition. He likes to hunt, but he also likes many other things. He is a powerful yet kind man. He built this wondrous city. He has brought roads, good order, and his love of art to Cathay. I have learned much from him."

"If that's Kublai Khan, then this must be China."

"I call it Cathay," said Marco. "Come. Let me take you to the bamboo pavilion for tea."

"I *am* thirsty," Lisa said, as they strolled to the pavilion.

"Be careful," said Marco, as he finished pouring Lisa some tea. "It's——"

Before Marco could finish his sentence, Lisa had picked up the steaming cup of tea.

"Eek!" she screeched, as she brought the cup to her lips. It was so hot, Lisa couldn't hold on. The cup fell to the floor and broke into bits.

"I'm so, so sorry." Lisa bent over to pick up the broken pieces. "You tried to warn me that it was hot."

Lisa looked more closely at the cup.

"It's funny. I know I've seen this pattern before. Yes!" Lisa exclaimed as she held a piece of the cup in her hand. "The trunk!"

"What trunk?" said Marco as his face began to stretch and bend. In no time, his words faded and the bamboo pavilion, with all its gilded columns and carved dragons, blurred into patches of swirling color.

"Oh, boy!" said Lisa, holding her stomach. "Here I go again!"

She was back. She slumped on her bed for a minute and then sat up and grabbed the journal.

Marco Polo and Kublai Khan

Marco Polo, son of a trader and explorer, joined his father and uncle on a journey to Cathay (what we now call China) in 1271. After three and a half years of treacherous travels, they finally reached their destination. Marco Polo spent the next fifteen years working for Kublai Khan, the Mongol Emperor who ruled Cathay. Marco Polo traveled all over. One of his favorite places was Shang-tu, better known as Xanadu. Here, Kublai Khan had built a magnificent palace surrounded by a beautiful walled garden. In the garden, wild animals and birds roamed and the emperor hunted them with falcons and cheetahs.

So the city she had seen was Xanadu, or Shang-tu, as Marco called it. It was beautiful and wild and enchanted! This whole adventure was amazing.

Excited, Lisa turned to the next page in the journal. Attached to the top were more puzzle pieces—a "T" and an "A."

"I-T-T-A. What is that? A name? A place? An animal?"

Lisa read on.

August 10, 1985

<u>Italy</u>

The Black Death! Even today those words make people tremble with fear. But in the 1300s, the Black Death was more than words. It was a terrible disease, some people called plague, that swept across Europe, killing millions. To our amazement, we've found something that did survive from those days—a handkerchief!

"The Black Death! Is that what Uncle Harold wants me to see next? Well I'm just not going! I don't want to see dead people.

"Maybe I can skip this century," thought Lisa.

Lisa tried to turn the journal page, but it wouldn't turn. She tried again to no avail. It was as if a powerful glue bound the pages together.

"I don't know how," thought Lisa, "but Uncle Harold has made sure I take this adventure century by century. He wants me to go to the 1300s. So, maybe I have to. After all, some people survived the Black Death. Maybe I'll meet a survivor."

Lisa sighed and stared at the beige cotton handkerchief

lying on top of the trunk. It was frayed and tattered, but there were delicate flowers stitched around the edges. Someone had taken great care to embroider the handkerchief.

"Okay, Uncle Harold," she suddenly decided, picking up the handkerchief. "I'm probably crazy, but here goes!"

Lisa rubbed her hand across the fine stitching. And, like Aladdin rubbing his lamp, she started the magic again.

Lisa was on the spin. To her relief, she hardly felt queasy anymore.

"I'm like a sailor getting his sea legs." She giggled, as colors and shapes flew past her like balloons in the wind.

And then, the spinning stopped.

*L*isa was standing in a deep valley surrounded by terraces of gnarled olive trees. The sun sparkled on the grass, the twisted trees, and Lisa's face. A large house stood nearby.

"This place doesn't look like death to me," thought Lisa.

She looked down at her clothes. Lisa wasn't wearing a fancy silk robe as she had in Marco Polo's time, just a rough linen dress. It looked as if it had been washed a hundred times. At least it wasn't itchy wool like the pants and tunic she'd worn on the Viking ship.

Lisa walked toward the house and saw a girl about her age lingering on the path. The girl was dressed in rags. Her hair was tangled. Her face was smudged with dirt.

"Hello," said Lisa. "My name is Lisa. What's yours?"

"Maria," said the girl softly. "I've been walking up and down here for a long time, trying to summon the courage to knock on the door. I hope they have food. I'm so hungry."

"Have you come from far away?" Lisa asked. She thought she recognized that the language the girl was speaking was Italian. Yes! "Italy" is what Uncle Harold's note said.

"I'm from a town near the port of Genoa. I've been walking for days. My family all died from the plague. My mother's last words to me were, 'Maria, run far away. Our town is full of death. Go to the country. There is health in the country'."

"I'm sorry about your family," said Lisa. "I wish I could give you food, but I don't have any."

"Maybe we can help each other. I will ask the people in this house if they will hire us to sew or clean."

Maria knocked, and after a moment a large, scowling woman opened the door.

"Go away, you filthy child," the woman barked at them.

"Please. I'm hungry," said Maria. "We want food, but not free food. We will work hard. Please give us a chance."

But before Maria could say another word, the woman pulled out a rough broom and began beating them away from the door.

"Go back to wherever you've come from. Go, before I set the dogs on you! My dogs are hungry also!"

Lisa and Maria began to run. They ran and ran until they were far away from the big house. Exhausted, they collapsed on a patch of soft grass.

"Hey, Maria—look! A river!" said Lisa.

Maria's sad eyes lit up.

"What luck! We can bathe. Then we can try another house. Perhaps if I'm cleaner, they'll think better of us," said Maria.

"Race you to the river, Maria."

In two leaps both girls were waist deep in the cool, clear water. They swam, splashed, and swam some more. For a while, time seemed to stand still. They were just two friends having fun on a beautiful summer morning.

Then Lisa felt something sharp pierce her leg.

"Ouch!" she cried.

"What's the matter?" asked Maria.

"I've scraped my leg on a rock. I think it's bleeding."

"Let's get out and look at it." Sure enough, Lisa's leg was gashed and bleeding.

Maria ran to a tree and ripped off four big leaves. Then she yanked a bunch of long grass from the riverbank and wrapped Lisa's leg.

"I don't know if it will hold, but try this for a while."

"Thanks," said Lisa, smiling gratefully at Maria. Maria smiled back. It was amazing! Maria looked like a different person. The clear river water had worked wonders. Her dress was still tattered but her face and hair shone.

"Can you walk, Lisa?" asked Maria. "I think we should try to find another house."

Lisa's leg still ached, but less.

"I'll try," she said. But a few steps later, Lisa felt something warm trickle down her leg again.

"Maria," she said. "I have to stop. My leg is still bleeding."

"Here," said Maria, reaching into her pocket. "This will help."

It was a handkerchief, stitched with delicate flowers around its edge.

"Oh, Maria, I can't take that. It's so pretty. I'll get blood all over it and ruin it."

"But you have to," said Maria. "You're my friend. Friends are more important than handkerchiefs." And without another word, Maria began wrapping the handkerchief around Lisa's bleeding leg.

Lisa sighed. She knew what was coming.

"Maria," she said quickly, "I'll never forget you." And as Lisa uttered the last word, the spinning began.

As soon as her dizziness stopped, Lisa grabbed the journal.

The Black Death

In the 1300s, the Italian city of Genoa was a thriving, busy port. Ships from all over sailed to and from Genoa. One of Genoa's main trading points was an Asian town called Caffa. The Black Death, or Plague, came to Genoa aboard a ship from Caffa. Rats carried fleas and fleas transmitted the Plague, although people at the time didn't know that.

The Plague spread across Europe, killing millions. The only way people found to control the Plague was to isolate people who were infected. Eventually the Plague died down but while it spread, death reigned across Europe.

Lisa felt a wave of sadness at the thought of Maria, wondering what had happened to her.

"Here we'd become friends and I just disappear. But Maria is tough. I know that somehow she survived. She had to."

Lisa turned the page. She held the next wooden puzzle piece. It was the letter "K."

"I-T-T-A-K," she said. "What does that mean?"

"This makes no sense. But Uncle Harold wants me to continue, and I have to trust him." Lisa read on in the journal.

Sept. 5, 1988

<u>Germany</u>

Unbelievable! We found a metal letter from 1454, from Johannes Gutenberg's first printing press—an invention that changed the world! Poor Gutenberg, he was embroiled in one lawsuit after another. All those lawsuits gave him endless aggravation.

Lisa picked up the metal piece from the printing press. It was the letter "L," in reverse.

She ran her finger over the bumpy metal letter. In no time, Lisa was spinning through time.

"Johannes Gutenberg, you are to appear in court." Two men stood facing each other in a doorway. One thrust a handwritten document into the other's hands.

"Good day, Sir," said the official, and left.

"How could he? How could he?" said Johannes pacing the hard wooden floor. "The Bible was almost finished!"

"Excuse me, Mr. Gutenberg," said Lisa.

"Who was that? Who said my name?" He spun around to stare at Lisa.

"My name is Lisa."

"Lisa? I don't think I know any Lisa, but never mind. Sit down. I'm about to have a cup of tea to settle my nerves and you can join me. I take it you've heard about the trial?"

"Only a little."

"I can scarcely believe it. For years I've been perfecting my printing press, an invention that will change books and reading forever. Can you imagine, for the first time people will not have to copy out words laboriously by hand. The printing press will make it possible to print hundreds, maybe thousands, of books. More people will learn how to read. It will open up a whole world of learning! I know it may be hard to believe."

"No, it's not," said Lisa.

"And now for the last few years, I have been slaving away, hour after hour, day after day, to produce the world's first printed Bible! Johannes Fust was my partner in this wonderful venture. I trusted him. And now he calls in his loan and takes me to court! And we are so close to finishing the Bible!"

Suddenly there was a sharp knock on the door.

Johannes leaped up. Fear crossed his face like a black shadow as he walked to the door. In a minute he was back.

"Thank goodness," he said, "I thought it was another official from the court, but it was only a peddler. I tell you, Lisa, there are days when I want to give up inventing. Days when I can't sleep for fear I will have no money left for food or clothing."

"Mr. Gutenberg," said Lisa, "you can't give up. Your invention is one of the greatest and most important ever. It's going to change the world."

Johannes Gutenberg's sad face broke into a small smile.

"Young lady, you are wise and kind beyond your years. Come. Let me show you something. I don't share this with many people."

As Lisa followed Mr. Gutenberg to a corner of the room, she quickly checked out her clothes. From one century to the next, she never knew what she'd be wearing. This time, it was a long, flowing dress.

"Here it is!" said Johannes, a broad smile grazing his face.

Lisa stared at the big clunky wooden and metal contraption. It looked like a bizarre modern art sculpture.

Johannes ran his hands lovingly across its frame.

"This," he said proudly, "is my printing press. And here," he said picking up a metal letter, "is one of my letters."

Before Lisa could protest, Mr. Gutenberg handed her the letter "L."

"Yes, 'L' for Lisa," he said, smiling. "Look at it. See how smooth——"

But Lisa never heard the rest of Johannes's sentence. She was spinning—twirling and twisting through time.

And then, Lisa was back beside the trunk. She read her uncle's entry.

Johannes Gutenberg and the Invention of the Printing Press

For a long time books were slowly and expensively printed by hand. Few books were produced and few people could afford them. Around 700 B.C., Chinese, Japanese, and Korean craftsmen made characters out of wood, tin, and porcelain to print. But these were often uneven or cracked. Then, in the middle of the 1400s, Johannes Gutenberg, a goldsmith and gemstone cutter, devised a mechanical way to print. He used his new invention to print the Bible, using metal letters. Gutenberg had many difficulties financing his invention, and some of his partners took him to court. Nevertheless, Gutenberg's invention made it possible for many more people to have access to books.

"Poor Mr. Gutenberg!" said Lisa. "He kept being dragged into court. But he never gave up, and in the end, the world knew who invented the printing press."

Lisa picked up the next two puzzle pieces—the letters "E" and "S."

"Yahoo! I have it," sang Lisa, dancing around the room. "It's not a name. It's not a place. It's two words. IT TAKES!"

Suddenly Lisa stopped dancing.

"But *what* does it take? Money? Time? People? I'm getting so close but I still don't understand what Uncle Harold is trying to tell me."

Lisa opened the journal and read on.

October 8, 1989

Poland

Out of this world! We found part of a manuscript written by the great Polish astronomer Nicolaus Copernicus! Copernicus studied and observed the planets for years, eventually reaching the conclusion that the earth was not the center of the universe. In those days, many people believed that the earth was at the center, and refused to listen to anything else. Some astronomers were even burned at the stake if they voiced their belief that this theory was untrue.

"Burned at the stake! Eeek!" A chill crawled up Lisa's spine.

What a horrible way to die! Was that what she was going to see in the 1500s? Did Copernicus get burned at the stake for his ideas?

"Maybe I should stop right now. I don't want to see anyone get burned. What if someone tries to burn me?" Lisa slammed the trunk shut.

"I'll just go and watch some TV," she decided. "I'll just forget all about this time travel stuff and stay right here in my nice safe house in my own century."

Lisa walked downstairs, but halfway down she stopped.

"Oh, I give up! I have to know what happens. And, anyway, Uncle Harold would never put me in any danger."

And with that, Lisa raced back upstairs, popped open the trunk, and saw a small yellowed piece of paper.

Lisa picked up the paper. As she stared at the faded numbers and drawings, the room began to blur.

"No, I can not write down my theories about the earth and the sun!" said an elderly man to his younger friend.

"See what my ideas have brought me? Nothing but pain, criticism, even the wrath of your Protestant thinker Martin Luther. He has great power and influence. He can ruin me! I am too old and too tired for arguments, prison, or—worse—being burned at the stake like a criminal."

The old man put his head in his hands and looked as if he might start weeping.

"But, Sir," said his young friend. "What you have discovered is the truth. The earth revolves around the sun, not the other way around. The truth can not be hidden. We have a responsibility to share our knowledge."

"At what cost, my dear Rhaeticus? My life? Yours? You are a Protestant. You must know the great risk you have taken by coming to see me. I am not only Roman Catholic, but a Catholic with new ideas about the universe."

"But I believe in what you have discovered, Nicolaus. It has nothing to do with religion. It's science."

Lisa stared at the two men. They were speaking so passionately they didn't notice her. But, suddenly, she felt a tickle in her throat and she couldn't stop herself. She coughed. Copernicus and Rhaeticus turned.

"Who are you?" asked Rhaeticus.

"Are you a spy for Martin Luther?" asked Copernicus.

"No, I've never met Martin Luther," said Lisa.

"She's just a child," said Rhaeticus.

"I may be a child," said Lisa, almost tripping on her wide skirt and pointy shoes, "but I took science and I know Nicolaus Copernicus is right. The earth is just one of the planets revolving around the sun."

"A girl studying science! Who teaches girls science?" said both men.

"I . . . I . . ." stammered Lisa, ". . . I go to a very unusual school. You've never heard of it, but we've heard about you."

"Do you hear, my dear Copernicus," said Rhaeticus excitedly. "Wise people all over the world are already learning about your theories. They too believe in them. Here, take the pen. Write it all down. You must!"

"Ssh," whispered Copernicus. "There's someone at the window. Martin Luther has spies everywhere. Quick, Rhaeticus, check."

Rhaeticus ran to the window and peered out. "It's just the wind rattling the trees, Copernicus," he said.

Copernicus took a deep breath and turned to Lisa. "These days, every sound makes me shake, every noise makes me quiver. I know people do not like new ideas—even if they are the truth. But I'm grateful my ideas impress you, young lady. And I must learn to be strong. I must. So, would you kindly bring me that paper on the table over there."

"Sure!" said Lisa, bouncing over to the heavy wooden table in the corner. "Is this what you want?" she said, picking up a manuscript filled with neat writing in a language she didn't recognize. She grabbed for a sheet of paper that came loose.

"Yes," said Copernicus. "It's my entire life's work written in Latin and now I must——"

But Lisa could only guess what Copernicus must do. The 1500s was rapidly blurring into a rainbow of colors.

Lisa picked up the journal. "Oh, I hope Nicolaus Copernicus and Rhaeticus didn't get burned for their ideas."

Nicolaus Copernicus

Nicolaus Copernicus was born in Poland in 1473. At Cracow University, he was taught the Ptolemic Theory, popular at the time, which said that the earth was the center of the universe. Copernicus became a church canon, but in his spare time he continued to observe and study astronomy. The more he learned, the more he believed the Ptolemic Theory was wrong.

Copernicus set down his theory in a little pamphlet, but he feared the negative reaction. The strongest criticism he received came from the Protestant thinker Martin Luther. Copernicus's young friend Rhaeticus encouraged him to explain his theories. Copernicus did publish again, in 1541. The book was officially printed in 1543, the year Copernicus died. In 1600 another scientist, Giordano Bruno, was burned at the stake for spreading the Copernican theory across Europe.

"Copernicus and Rhaeticus weren't burned, but Giordano Bruno was!" said Lisa shivering. "How could people be burned for their ideas!"

Lisa picked up the next puzzle pieces—"U" and "R."

"IT TAKES U-R?" she said. "What does 'UR' mean?"

Lisa read on in the journal.

March 9, 1990

<u>India</u>

Astounding! India! The Taj Mahal! What beauty Emperor Shah Jahan created in the mid-1600s. It's more magnificent and luminous than any picture could convey. And to find a gleaming black tile intact is wondrous. It must have been unused in the final construction.

"The Taj Mahal! Wow!" said Lisa. "Nothing could be dangerous about that beautiful building!"

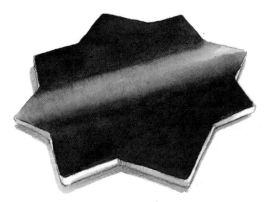

Lisa ran her fingers across the shimmering piece of tile. "India—here I come," she said as the spinning began.

When it stopped, Lisa couldn't believe what she saw. It was the Taj Mahal, but it was not yet completed. The beautiful building was still being built. People buzzed around hauling, lifting, and cutting great slabs of cream-colored marble.

In pictures, the area around the Taj Mahal looked silent and serene. But here, it was bustling and busy with workers.

"Stop gawking, you fool," an angry man shouted at Lisa.

Lisa quickly looked down. She was dressed in baggy old pants like a boy.

"You'd better get back to work or you'll lose your job," said a boy about Lisa's age. His eyes were tired, like the eyes of a sad old man. His clothes were torn and dirty. His hands were scratched and bruised.

"Why are you working here? You're just a kid," said Lisa. "Aren't there laws against children working?"

The boy laughed sadly. "Laws?" he said. "There is only one law—if you don't work, you don't eat. If I don't work, my family starves."

"What about your father?" asked Lisa.

For a minute the boy said nothing.

"My father is dead," he finally muttered, his voice cracking like clay. "A slab of marble fell on him at work. Now I must haul marble in his place."

"Stop jabbering!" yelled the overseer, boxing the boy's ears.

"How could you! He wasn't doing anything," Lisa shouted.

"How dare you speak to me like that," yelled the man, his
face bright red with fury.

"Run," whimpered the boy. "Run."

Run? Where? Everything was open space around the
construction site—everything except the dump. It was full of
stuff. There had to be somewhere to hide there.

So Lisa ran as fast as she could toward the dump.

"Stop, wicked boy!" screamed the man.

Lisa could hear him cursing as he ran after her. She
smelled the dump even before she reached it. It reeked of
rotten food, vegetables, and dead animals.

Lisa felt sick to her stomach. There was so much garbage
piled like mountains all around the dump that there was no

place to run. And a giant rat just stood there on a pile of refuse, staring as if he was going to leap right into her face!

Where was the black tile to get her home? Lisa looked around frantically but all she could see was garbage and the rat's hungry eyes.

And then, Lisa heard the man's voice right behind her!

"There you are, insolent scoundrel!" he shouted in a fearsome voice. He was only a step away from her.

Startled at the shouting, the rat scampered off the pile. Where the rat had stood lay the black tile, glistening like glass. Lisa grabbed the tile just as the overseer grabbed her hair.

"Ouch!" she yelped.

She could still feel the painful yank as she spun.

"Phew! That was close!" she said, rubbing her sore scalp. Lisa took a deep breath and picked up the journal.

The Taj Mahal

The Taj Mahal was built in India by Shah Jahan in the mid-1600s as a memorial to his favorite wife, Mumtaz Mahal. Mumtaz died in childbirth while accompanying her husband on a military campaign. The distraught Shah vowed to build her a magnificent tomb. To do so, Shah Jahan gathered the greatest architects and craftsmen. These designers brought together the finest marble, jade, crystal, gems, and stones and began to build. Construction of the Taj Mahal began in 1632. It took 22 years to complete and 20,000 workers.

"So the Taj Mahal is a tomb, which took lots of work and many people to build," thought Lisa. "I hope that boy didn't get into trouble from that awful man. I hope he didn't have a terrible life. Why do children have to work so hard? Even today there are places where children are made to work like slaves."

Lisa picked up the next puzzle piece and stared at it.

"'E.' IT TAKES U-R-E. What does that mean? Is it some kind of code? Uncle Harold, what are you trying to tell me?"

"Phone, Lisa!" Lisa's mother's voice broke into her thoughts.

Lisa slammed the trunk closed and ran to the phone. It was her best friend, Pam.

"Hi, Lisa. What's new?"

For a moment, Lisa hesitated. She wanted to tell someone about the trunk. And Pam was her best friend. They always told each other everything.

"If I tell you what's new, will you promise not to laugh?" asked Lisa.

"Sure," said Pam.

"I've just been to the 1600s and watched the Taj Mahal being built."

"Huh?" said Pam.

"I have a magic trunk that Uncle Harold sent me before he died and I've been time-traveling through the centuries all morning. Uncle Harold has sent me on a quest. Pam? Are you there?"

"I'm here but is this some kind of silly joke, Lisa? I promised I wouldn't laugh, and I haven't, but really."

"Pam. I'm telling the truth, I promise."

"Yeah. Sure. And I'm the Empress of China. I'll call you later, after you've had a nap or something."

And with that, Pam hung up.

"If my best friend won't believe me, no one will," thought Lisa miserably.

"Now what?" Lisa closed her eyes and tried to think. "Should I go on or stop? My head still hurts from that awful man pulling my hair. My leg is still sore from that rock in the 1300s. What if in the next century someone does something worse?"

Lisa shuddered at the thought.

"Uncle Harold wouldn't let that happen. I just know it," she reassured herself.

Slowly, Lisa went back to her room.

Lisa opened the trunk again.

April 8, 1991

<u>Canada</u>

What a discovery! A rare map of the Canadian prairies drawn by explorer, surveyor, and mapmaker David Thompson. Setting out in August 1797, Thompson traveled in a large canoe from Lake Superior to the Lake of the Woods. He explored, and drew the first reliable maps of, many areas in Canada.

"Well, that sounds more like it! Sitting in a lovely big canoe, dipping my hand into a clear lake, exploring beautiful new lands. That's what I call a trip!"

Lisa picked up the map and the spinning began.

"Hey, I can't see," Lisa shouted. "And it's freezing. I thought this was supposed to be August."

"It was August when we started out," called a voice. "But it's deep December now."

Lisa glanced at her clothes. She was wrapped in fur, but she was still shivering.

"Oh, no!" groaned Lisa. "December. Snow!"

"And ice and cold and misery," said the voice. "Who's speaking? In all this blinding snow, I can't see you."

"My name is Lisa. Who are you?"

"David Thompson. Try and stay within range of my voice, Lisa. It's easy to get lost in this blizzard. One of our men has already disappeared into the snow and we fear for his life."

"Can't we build a fire or something?" Lisa asked, shivering. "I feel like an iceberg. My feet feel like they're going to drop off from the cold."

"We're trying to build a fire," said David Thompson, "but it's hard finding wood and lighting a fire in all this wet snow. As soon as we're able, we'll get a fire going and cook some buffalo meat for dinner."

"Buffalo meat?" Lisa gulped. "I guess it's like hamburger," she told herself.

"We must eat what we can find," said David Thompson. "If we ever find our way back home, the first thing I will do is enjoy a very large, very hot meal, served at a table."

"What do you mean, 'if'?" said Lisa.

"You never know in the wilderness. If it's not bone-chilling weather, it's a wild river, or miserable disease, or bad food. If it wasn't for the kindness and help of the Chipewyan people, I'd surely have died two years ago near Athabasca. And this storm is one of the worst I've seen. I was hoping to take my maps back and show everyone how vast and wonderful this new land is. I've packed my maps carefully, but this snow is so wet. I fear they will be destroyed."

Lisa felt a wet glove on her shoulder. "Lisa, could you hold this map for a second. I must find something to protect it."

Before Lisa could say anything, David Thompson handed her a packet. As soon as Lisa touched it, she knew what was going to happen.

"Goodbye, Mr. Thompson. I hope you get back——" she called as the spinning began.

"**M**mmm," said Lisa, crawling under her warm, cozy quilt. "It's so nice and warm here." Snuggling deeper, she began to read.

David Thompson

David Thompson was an explorer, surveyor, trader, and map maker. He was the first European to travel down the Columbia River to the Pacific Ocean. In 1797, he began to explore the area around Lake Superior. Starting in August, Thompson and his party, with the help of native guides, traveled comfortably in a large canoe. Eager to continue, they kept going through November and December, despite the hazardous winter conditions. By December, Thompson and his men were stranded by a terrible blizzard. One of their party was lost for a while. He was found later, cold but alive.

After many years of travel and surveying, Thompson produced maps so accurate they serve as the basis for maps to this day. Thompson died in poverty, unaware of his lasting contribution.

"Wow! Mr. Thompson did bring his maps back to show people, but he never realized how incredibly valuable they were to explorers after him. It's not fair when people die before they know that their work is important. But at least he didn't freeze to death, like some explorers did."

Lisa shivered at the memory of the blizzard. Then she picked up the next puzzle pieces. They were the letters "A" and "G."

"IT TAKES U-R-E-A-G? What kind of weird message is that? Oh, well. I guess it's on to the 1800s!"

Lisa felt a rush of excitement. Despite all the crazy, dangerous places she'd visited, she was having the time of her life. And she couldn't wait to see where she was going next.

Lisa flipped the page.

May 7, 1992

<u>Turkey</u>

We found a lamp from Florence Nightingale's time. Could it have been one of the lamps she actually used at the Scutari Hospital during the Crimean War of the 1850s? Male doctors and officials resisted her efforts to clean up the dirty, rat-infested hospital near Constantinople, but she never gave up.

"Rats! Not again! And a filthy hospital in a bloody war zone. Why can't Uncle Harold send me to a nice beach with swaying palm trees instead of swaying sick soldiers?"

For a moment Lisa imagined herself on a beautiful, sunny beach. Then she stared at the rusty old lamp.

"Only two more centuries to go, and two more clues to find," she said. "How bad can the Crimea be? Well, I guess I'll find out."

And with that, Lisa picked up the lamp and rubbed it.

When Lisa stopped spinning, she found herself in pitch darkness. Not a light flickered. Not a sound could be heard.

"Is anyone here?" Lisa whispered.

No one answered.

Lisa took a small step to the right.

"Hello?" she called out.

No one answered.

The dark was as thick as fog. And the silence was eerie. Suddenly, Lisa thought she heard faint footsteps. Where did they come from? The right? The left? Lisa listened again. Yes, definitely, the left.

Lisa spun around in the direction of the footsteps and, clunk, bumped smack into a woman.

"I'm sorry," Lisa murmured, rubbing her sore head.

Lisa stared at the woman. She looked as if she was not only in pain, but annoyed. She was wearing a long, gray uniform with a little cap on her head. And . . . she held a lamp!

"Florence Nightingale!" Lisa exclaimed.

"Yes, young lady," said Florence Nightingale sternly. "That's who I am. Who are you and why are you wandering around at this time of night? If you're one of the new nurses, you should be in bed. Sleeping. These poor men need a nurse who's alert."

Lisa glanced down at her clothes. She was wearing a long gray uniform just like Florence Nightingale's.

"I . . . I . . . don't know where my bed is," Lisa finally mumbled.

"How long have you been here?" Miss Nightingale asked sharply.

"Not long," said Lisa.

"Well, follow me, but I have more important things to do than squire forgetful nurses to their quarters. So pay attention as we go."

Lisa followed Florence Nightingale into a building and down a long, dark hall. As they walked, the hall filled up with a dank, foul stench. The stench grew stronger and stronger. Soon it was so awful Lisa felt her stomach heave. But the horrible odor didn't bother Florence Nightingale.

Florence lifted her lamp. Its light shone on the face of a young soldier. His legs were wrapped in dirty cloths, stained with blood. He moaned and winced as he tossed on the narrow cot.

"Miss Nightingale," he whispered, "you're here."

Florence Nightingale reached for the young soldier's hand and squeezed it gently.

"How are you, Jack?" she said in a voice so soft and kind, Lisa could hardly believe it came from the same woman who'd barked at her just a few minutes ago. Florence Nightingale spoke to the wounded soldier, comforting him, promising to change his dressing and make him more comfortable.

Jack smiled through his pain-wracked face.

Suddenly, Florence turned to Lisa. "Here, nurse, hold my lamp. I'm going to change Jack's dressing."

And before Lisa could say anything, Florence Nightingale thrust the lamp into her hands.

The last words Lisa heard, in Jack's raspy whisper, were, "Thank you. Thank you both."

And then Lisa was back. She ran to her window and flung it open, breathing in the fresh air deeply, like a desert traveler gulping down water. What a relief to be away from that horrible hospital. Yet, how brave Florence Nightingale and all those nurses were to live with the stink, the sadness, and the limited supplies to help those poor soldiers.

Quickly, Lisa turned to the journal and read.

Florence Nightingale

Florence Nightingale was born to a wealthy English family. Her parents wanted her to grow up as a typical wealthy young woman of the times, attending parties, traveling, and marrying a rich man. But Florence wanted to help the sick and unfortunate. Despite her family's opposition, Florence went to nursing school in Germany. By the time she was 33, she became the superintendent of a woman's hospital in London.

When Britain and France went to war with Russia in the Crimea in 1854, Florence Nightingale was asked to take charge of nursing at the hospital in Scutari, Constantinople (now Istanbul, Turkey). The conditions at the hospital were terrible and Florence received enormous resistance from the doctors and officials at the hospital, who resented the "dictatorship of a woman." Gradually, though, they came to admire her organization, common sense, and resilience—as did the whole British nation.

"Wow! Florence Nightingale was tough, bossy, but wonderful too."

Lisa picked up the next puzzle piece. "O."

"IT TAKES U-R-E-A-G-O. What *is* this? The next century has to have the answer."

Lisa turned the page.

June 5, 1994

<u>United States of America</u>

Wonderful! We found a touching school essay called "My Mother, My Hero" by a ten-year-old Montgomery, Alabama, black girl named Millie Reed. Millie wrote the essay in 1955, when black citizens (who were referred to then as Negroes or colored people) were campaigning to have the same rights as white citizens. The black citizens of Montgomery refused to ride the buses as a protest against segregation and the arrest of Rosa Parks, who had refused to give up her bus seat to a white man.

"Wow!" said Lisa. "I remember seeing Rosa Parks on TV. She's in her eighties now. It will be fun to meet a girl from the 1950s. So, last clue, here I come!"

Lisa fingered Millie's yellowing essay and immediately began to spin.

*L*isa shivered and snuggled deeper into her hooded jacket. She was standing on a sidewalk in cold, pelting rain.

"Boy, am I glad Uncle Harold provided a waterproof jacket for this adventure. I'd be a wet rag otherwise," she thought.

Lisa glanced down the street. To her left, a black woman and her young daughter clung to an umbrella as they walked.

"Oh, Mama, I'm so tired," the girl complained.

"I know, Millie," said her mother.

"Mama," said Millie, "couldn't we take the bus just this once? It's pouring rain and we're still miles from home."

"No, Millie. We can not take the bus. We can not break the boycott. A boycott only works if people band together. There are a lot of tired Negroes walking home from work tonight, walking for justice. We can't let them down."

Millie sighed. "I guess you're right, Mama."

"Hey, you," shouted a white man driving by in a long blue car. "Why don't you take the bus like normal people? No one cares about your stupid boycott. We got laws in Alabama."

Millie and her mom ignored the man and kept walking.

A black sedan drove up slowly and then, with a screech, accelerated, sending waves of dirty gutter water at Millie and her mother.

The man in the sedan rolled down his window and laughed. "Enjoy your boycott!" he screamed and drove off.

Millie's mother pulled a handkerchief out of her purse and softly rubbed Millie's mud-streaked face. Lisa could hear Millie sobbing quietly.

Lisa was stunned. How could those men be so cruel? Millie and her mom weren't hurting anyone. They were just standing up for their rights.

But before Lisa could do or say anything, they began to cross the street. Suddenly, the black sedan was back. But this time, it was heading straight for Millie and her mother!

"Watch out, Millie!" screamed Lisa.

Just in time, Millie's mom grabbed Millie's hand and dashed to the safety of the sidewalk. The sedan disappeared into the rainy mist like an evil apparition. Millie's mother leaned against a building and closed her eyes. Millie still held her mother's hand.

"Can I help?" Lisa asked, as she walked toward them.

"You've helped already," said Millie's mother, her voice filled with heavy sadness. "We can't thank you enough for warning us about that crazy driver. It's good to know that not all white folks hate us—so much they would even want to kill us."

"But how did you know my name?" Millie asked, drying her eyes.

"I . . . I . . . I saw it on your bag," said Lisa, pointing to the back of Millie's school bag.

"You sure have good eyesight," said Millie.

"20/20," said Lisa laughing.

Millie and her mother smiled.

"I want you to know, I think your protest is right and brave," said Lisa.

"Thank you," said Millie's mom.

"Do you want to see my essay for school about my mama?" asked Millie. "I just got it back today. I was going to show you at home, Mama. I got an 'A.' Here, read it."

And before Lisa knew it, Millie had thrust the neatly written essay into her hand.

"Oh, Millie," said Lisa quickly. "Things will get better."

Lisa didn't know if Millie and her mother heard her last words as she spun forward in time.

As soon as she was back in her room, Lisa grabbed Uncle Harold's journal and read.

My Mother, My Hero

by Millie Reed

My mama is not famous. She is not rich. She is a seamstress and she works hard every day making nice clothes.

Every day after school, Mama picks me up and we take the bus home together, make supper, and talk. Then I do my homework. Mama wants me to learn everything I can and get a good education so I can become anything I want when I grow up.

For the last month, Mama and I have not taken the bus home because we are protesting the law that says Negroes must ride in the back of the bus. Rosa Parks was the first to protest and she was arrested. Now we're all supporting her.

"Miss Parks was brave and we have to be brave with her," Mama told me. "We will not take the buses in Montgomery until the laws are changed and all people, no matter what color they are, have the same rights."

My mama is tired after work, but she still walks home every day. I know she will walk as long as it takes to get justice.

I will walk beside her.

"That is 'A' work, Millie! And together you changed the law," said Lisa, smiling.

"And now for the last part of the puzzle!"

Lisa's hands shook as she turned the page. There it was! The last piece. The letter "C."

"'C'? IT TAKES U-R-E-A-G-O-C. That makes no sense. Wait—there's a note."

Dear Lisa,

This journey is over. Be guided by what you have seen and what you have felt. And remember: Always look beyond the jumble.

Love,

Uncle Harold

"Always look beyond the jumble? What kind of clue is that?" Lisa slammed the trunk shut and sat down on her bed. "It can't just be jumbled letters. . . . Or can it? Yes! That's it. Jumbled letters! The letters are scrambled like a code!"

Lisa tried to think of a word beginning with the "R." It didn't work. She tried a "G," but it didn't work either.

"How about 'C'? Yes, that's it! I've got it! CO- COUR- Yes! Of course! It's COURAGE!"

Lisa leaped off the bed and laid out all the letter tiles in the correct order on the floor.

"That's the message! It takes courage to sail stormy seas like Leif Eriksson. It takes courage to save your village like Sarah. It takes courage to start again after losing your whole family like Maria. It takes courage to trek through unknown lands and danger like Marco Polo. It takes courage to keep inventing while fighting problems every day like Gutenberg. It takes courage to tell the world your theories, even though you risk death, like Copernicus. It takes courage to do backbreaking work to support your family, and somehow endure, like the boy at the Taj Mahal. It takes courage to explore vast new frontiers like David Thompson. It takes courage to fight your family's and society's disapproval like Florence Nightingale. It takes courage to stand up for your rights like Millie and her mom did.

"Oh, Uncle Harold. That's it! That's what you were trying to tell me. Life takes courage."

Lisa looked in the trunk and sighed. She was glad she'd figured the puzzle out, but this great adventure was now over.

All the trunk's objects lay on her bed. Somehow Lisa knew they were now just relics of the past. All their magic was gone. The trunk was empty now except . . . there was still something stuck in a corner. It was a small tag.

Lisa read it.

"It's about me!" she exclaimed.

The tag said "Lisa, 2000 A.D."

Uncle Harold wanted her to add something to the trunk. Something about her. Something special. But what?

And then, as sure as she knew her name, Lisa knew. She pulled out her collection of buttons from the bottom drawer of her dresser. It didn't take long to find the button she wanted and attach it to the tag.

That would take courage. Lots of courage. A new millennium and a new journey were beginning.